THE MARY B CHRONICLES

THE LONG WAY AROUND BOOK 4

DAKIARA

MIND FLOW PUBLISHING & PRODUCTION LLC PRESENTS

First Printing: 2020

ISBN 978-1-951271-08-4 Paperback

ISBN 978-1-951271-09-1 Ebook

Additional copies of this book and others are available by mail or by visiting the website listed below. Check website for pricing.

Mind Flow Publishing & Production LLC

PO Box 48768 Cumberland, North Carolina 28331-8768

www.mindflowpublishingproduction.com

Cover design by Carrie & Co.

Editing by Stories Matter Editing

Formatting Design by Covers My Way

Thank you for helping to bring Mary B to Life......

DEDICATED TO MY LOVES

DAQUAN, DEJA, DANTE

KEVONN AND KIARA

**RIP
DAQUAN JAMIQUE 95
&
KIARA DENISE 00**

Special Thanks
To GOD for Giving Me
The Strength and The Words
To Do This Project.
Blessed by The Experiences to Draw From
It Has Not Always Been Easy.

Dedicated to Some Who Have Gone Before Me
**Mary Merriman
Naomi Thompson**

PROLOGUE

Bo was indeed still in town. He kept his distance from Janet; he didn't want to scare her. He made it his business to learn her schedule, and he was content just watching her for the time being. He knew enough to know she wasn't dating anyone; she did go to the gun range a lot. She was spending a lot of time with that chick he seen her with that night at the restaurant.

He remembered their life a little differently than Janet. Bo had been super aggressive, but it didn't start out that way. When the two of them met, he was immediately taken by her. Janet had a smile to die for. He showed her that he was a good man by constantly showering her with his affection and gifts. Bo would always bring her flowers to her job, or to her client's house it didn't matter where she was, he wanted to make sure she knew he loved her.

Bo grew up with a dad who was in and out of jail, so he barely knew him. He just knew enough to know he didn't want to be anything like him. The sad thing was, he was more like him then he could have ever imagined.

Bo never meant to hurt Janet. He loved her and he just got upset when he thought someone else wanted her. He kept telling himself that he needed to get help, but it wasn't until he nearly killed her the last time, that he realized he had gone too far. He was out of control and he lost the one person he knew he could count on. Bo wanted Janet back and he felt that he could get her to take him back, but it was going to require patience. That was not his best quality, but he was determined to get her back or die trying.

CHAPTER ONE

JEAN WAS NOT OVERLY EXCITED ABOUT HER BROTHER moving away, but she understood why it needed to happen. She was happy that Davina did consult with her and Mary B before she made the final decision. Jean of all people knew she didn't have to. The two of them had been through their share of ups and downs when it came to Robert. Jean was sure that Davina loved him with all her heart and that was enough for her to want to make sure he wasn't feeling guilty about leaving. Jean told him that it was only two hours away, she would bring Mary B to visit as often as she or he liked. It would definitely be a change from seeing your family almost every day, but Jean knew that everyone would be okay and adjust to the new normal, eventually.

With Davina and Robert moving that would give them all somewhere to go and visit, perhaps drop the children off and enjoy a night on the town. Since Christian was staying with them he had been a great help. He helped with the twins, so that Jean could make sure the two little ladies were good. Jean thought it funny how Tim and Christian fussed over who was going to spend time with the children almost on a daily basis. The children definitely didn't feel unloved.

Miles was still Miles; he was right there keeping an eye on Raven. He would often miss time with the boys because he was on guard duty. Miles didn't seem to mind one bit, he loved spending time with his sister. Life was going in the right direction for everyone it seemed.

MARY B WAS EXCITED ABOUT THE WAY THINGS WERE going with the family. Janet the newest addition had opted to stay in town instead of running off. Jean and Tim were doing well, all of the children were healthy and coming along really well. Davina and Robert were moving a short distance away, but it was time for him to strike out on his own. He had felt obligated to stay and take care of the family. He had fulfilled his obligation and now he was obligated to see to it that his family came first. There had been a lot of sacrifice in this family over the years and Mary B was excited about the celebrations that were coming. Lord only knew that this family had been through the fire and back again. Through it all they always managed to make it through just a little stronger than the week or day before.

William had been battling with his health lately, but of course the children didn't know that, and they never would as long as he had it his way.

The next few weeks went by pretty quickly. Davina and Robert were getting settled into their new house. Davina hadn't played around; the movers were there at the house that very weekend after they saw the new place. Robert had left and went to work that day and by the time he came back the house was just about packed up.

The following Monday morning a cleaning crew came in and did a full cleaning of the house from top to bottom. The painters arrived on Tuesday; she didn't want the landlord to have anything to say about how the house was left. By the weekend they were in their new home. She had found a few locations for her boutique. She just needed to get to work on some designs. She was planning on having something's ready by March of the New Year.

Davina was proud of herself, she had put in a lot of hard work lately, and it was finally paying off. The children were adjusting well to new place. They have made a few friends that lived a few houses down. Every afternoon they would go to the park together. Davina had also made some friends, which was one thing that she didn't have many of. It kind of made her miss being around Jean and Janet all the time. Robert was adjusting; he hadn't found a job yet, but he had a few offers, the commute wasn't too bad, he would have to drive about thirty minutes each way. He wasn't too fond of that idea, but he knew he would have to get a job soon. Although he loved his wife and loved spending time with her and the children, he didn't like feeling as if he was just loafing. He had never been a lazy man and he didn't want Davina to feel like she had to take care of him.

Over the following weeks Davina sensed that Robert was a little uneasy. "Hey you, what's wrong? You should be happy. You have a wonderful wife and beautiful kids, a new house and a fresh start. You can do whatever you want. So, what will make you happy my love?"

Robert didn't want to appear to be ungrateful or

unhappy. "I'm sorry Vina, it's just that I'm not used to sitting around. I love spending time with you and the children, but I have to find a job soon. I don't want you to think that I'm just being lazy."

"Babe remember that this was all my idea. So why would I think you are just being lazy? Remember you took care of us for all these years, no questions asked. So just accept that I want to do something nice for you. Yes, I know your pride is out of this world. I just want you to be happy, not just working because you have to. Do you remember you used to play several instruments in school? You always seemed happy when you played for me. Maybe you could do something with music?" Davina knew in her heart this was the right thing. She just hoped Robert thought so too.

"That's because I was playing for you. Davina you inspired me. You always have. You inspire me to be a better man, not just for me, but for us. I want the children to have a positive role model to look up to, and not just because I'm their father."

Davina understood where he was coming from. She even admired him for it, but it still didn't stop her from wanting him to enjoy the life they have been given. "Babe, what if you worked on your music? You used to write songs, I recall you wrote a few about me," Davina laughed out loud.

Robert shrugged the thought away. "You know how long it's been since I've written or even played music. I wouldn't know where to begin. I don't mean to be a spoilsport, but I promise you babe, I will figure it out. I love you for what you did, well what you are still doing for our family." Davina hugged him and told him, he had time, and there was no rush. "We do need to plan this New Year's Eve Party though. So, get to planning sir."

"I can do that. Yeah, I can do that. It is going to be crazy with everyone wanting to drop in and see our new place." Davina hadn't seen him this excited in a bit. She went with it. It was good to see him finally smiling and excited about having a project.

As the days went on and preparations for the party were coming together, Davina was taking her time with putting up the boxes from their move. Going through the boxes she saw a lot of their lives together captured in the photos. She saw the box labeled Mom, inside was a few pictures that she managed to save of her mom. There were even a few of her mom and Bobby. The ones she liked most, were the ones where her mom was pregnant, they looked happy. There was a hint of something familiar when she looked at the pictures. Davina shook it off though. She thought she was just being overly emotional, with moving into a new home and the new start and everything that was going on with Robert.

At that moment Davina thought about Janet, she missed having her around. She made a point to call her and invite her to stay for a few days, just to get out of town. Change of scenery couldn't do any harm.

Those were Janet's thoughts exactly when she received the call from Davina. She was actually happy to get away, she was starting to get paranoid thinking Bo was watching her every move. She would stay away from home as much as possible, and she started leaving all the lights on in her apartment. She knew it was crazy, because she knew if he wanted to get to her, he would, and nothing was going to stop him. She didn't want to say anything, but she knew that Tim,

William, and even Christian had all taken turns keeping an eye on her and had been driving by her apartment. She knew it was to check on her, and she truly hated that they felt they had to. They were following Mary B's strict orders, and they dared not to disobey her. Janet thought what better way to give the fellas a break than to go and stay with Davina for a few days.

Mary B agreed that it was a good choice. She had William drive Janet, so that way he could make sure they weren't being followed. William always carried Lucy Pearl with him, although he hadn't actually used it in a while, he was still an amazing shot. Mary B gave him the hardest time about having that gun. He would always taunt her and say that he was a man and he was supposed to have one. She would tease him and tell him that he would end up shooting his foot off or something, before he actually shot someone else.

Janet's stay with Davina and Robert was only to last a few days, but instead it turned into over a month. She had truly missed being around the children. From the looks of it they had missed her too. It was like a sleepover every night. Being there with them made her forget about Bo for a while. She was actually able to sleep, something she hadn't really done much of since running into Bo at the restaurant. Janet helped Robert work on the New Year's Eve party plans while she was there. She had even gone and looked at a few apartments in the area, you know just in case. Janet had become very fond of this town, they had a gun range, and a kick boxing class close by.

A week before the party she asked William if he would come get her, she felt it was time to go back home. William didn't hesitate, he hung up the phone and he left almost immediately. Before long they were walking into her apartment. William wanted to do a walk through just to make sure that everything was good, and it was. Before leaving, he asked if she was okay, or needed anything. She told him she was good. Janet told him she would see him at the party if not before and not to worry about her, she was going to be just fine.

Janet decided that she would go ahead and make sure the offer to be on the hospital staff was still open. She felt it was time to go back to work, and she felt she was ready. While out for a jog her second day back at home, she noticed a car that seemed to be following her. At first, she thought it was all in her head and she was simply being paranoid. She was relieved when she made her turn to jog down the trail, which was off road, like she normally did, the car stopped not far ahead of where she turned. She could hear them backing up. She kept running. Janet thought perhaps they had made the wrong turn and merely turned around. By the time she made it to the end of the trail, she saw the car pass her by; they didn't stop, so again she thought nothing of it. Janet decided to change up her route just in case. She didn't want to be out running in any secluded areas, you know just in case.

She would later mention this to Mary B, who suggested she not run outdoors at all at least for a while. "Besides, it's too cold to be doing all that running outside. You're going to catch a cold or the flu."

"Yeah you have to be related to my mom, she fussed about the same things when I was a child. You actually do favor a bit, it's crazy because I never noticed it before. It's funny how knowing something makes you see things in a whole different light." Janet said as she clasped Mary B's hand.

The next few days were pretty uneventful. Everyone was excited about the party that was coming up that weekend. The plan was that everyone would drive up to Robert's sometime on Saturday and stay until Dick Clark dropped the ball that Sunday night, well Monday morning. The family had the option of staying over on Monday as well, but they figured that Tim and Jean wouldn't because the children had school on Tuesday.

Davina had really planned out a nice evening. Robert helped a little with the decorations, but he left most of the work to Davina. She didn't mind too much. After being stuck in a wheelchair, she was excited to be able to be back to her old self. She was determined that it was going to be a good weekend.

Tim and Jean and their kids arrived around lunchtime. The next to arrive were William and Mary B; they brought Janet with them so she wouldn't have to drive alone, although it was only a few hours. Janet told them they didn't have to keep babying her, but she secretly loved it. It had been a long time since anyone had made her feel loved. The weekend was going along so well that they all agreed to make it a family tradition. They would alternate between Robert, Jean, and Mary B's houses each year. They even joked that maybe the children would keep it going when they got older.

Tim chimed in that the girls would probably do it, but the boys, who knew what they would be up to? They would probably be chasing behind some women. Everyone laughed at that thought. Miles was already a cutie, as well as

Dayshaun. Kevin and Joseph were quiet, but they too liked the ladies. Jean sighed; she knew she was going to have a time on her hands with all of them once they got a little older. Thank goodness for Tim being there.

On Sunday evening Janet's phone rang, and it showed a private number. This was the first time it had done it in a while. Janet let it go to voicemail just like the others. She knew there wasn't going to be a message, there never was. Just then her phone vibrated with a message, which simply said, *I miss you.* Again, the number did not show up. In her mind she knew who it was of course. There weren't many options.

She shook her head, and Robert was the first to ask what was wrong. She just showed him her phone. "This is just getting ridiculous now. What does he want?" Janet knew that answer was just as simple. He wanted her, whether it was to be with or hurt her she wasn't sure, he was obsessed with her.

Mary B suggested that first thing Tuesday, she get her number changed, and be very selective as to who got the number from that point on. Janet had fully intended to change the number but got busy with Davina and getting to know the family and it slipped her mind. Janet agreed but in the back of her mind she knew, that wouldn't stop him. Nothing was going to stop him until he had her in his clutches. She was honestly surprised that he had been this quiet for so long. Even though she tried not to think about him lurking around, she still jumped when someone was too close to her. She still had the dreams that he would get to her. Janet had kept those details from the family. She didn't want them to worry. She turned her phone off and the family tried to salvage the rest of the evening.

Mary B turned the TV up so they could see Dick Clark was on, everyone had been so focused on Janet, that they hadn't realized that it was already 11:30 pm. They flashed to a picture of the ball, and Joseph got excited. His mom had told him they were going to be dropping a pretty ball that was huge. His excitement turned everyone's focus to the TV.

Watching *Dick Clark's Rocking New Year's Eve* was a family tradition with Robert and Jean, from the time they were three years old. They loved watching the ball drop and they were back together again, and it always seemed to make their parents happy. Everyone had a disposable camera, even the children; their job was to take pictures whenever they wanted. The purpose of the cameras was so that no matter where life took them, they would always have these memories. And that night they made plenty. Jean couldn't wait to get the pictures developed, to see just what everyone saw that night. Robert had given her a hard time about going out and getting all the cameras. He said the guy at the drugstore acted like he was some kind of creeper. In the end it would be a decision that they didn't regret.

CHAPTER TWO

When Janet turned her phone off, she didn't know that she had received about ten more phone calls. She knew it was about ten, because this time he left messages after each call. Janet turned the phone on about 1 am, and it went off in a constant barrage of notifications while the messages were coming through.

Mary B and William were getting ready to head back home. Mary had promised to take one of her friends from the church to the store. They asked if Janet was catching a ride back home with them, she told them she was going to stay for a day or so. She wanted to enjoy her freedom before she went back to work. Once they saw Mary B and William off, Janet decided to listen to the messages.

The first one made her remember what it was like in the beginning with Bo. The kinder gentler man she fell in love with, but as she got further into the voicemails, he seemed more agitated that she didn't answer, and what made it worse was that he said he knew she must have turned the phone off, because it was going straight to voicemail. "Janet I just wanted to tell you I love you. I wanted to tell you to have a happy new year."

By the last call he was heated, and completely unrecognizable as the man who called and left the first message. "Look I know things went bad for us. I thought we could start over. I just want to show you that I love you and there will never be anyone who can love you more than I do. This is pretty disrespectful that you can't even answer my calls. You do know that I know where you are at this very moment. I know that you sometimes ride in that old 1967 Shelby. Nothing will keep me from you, nothing and no one, you'd do well to remember that Janet." And with that he hung up the phone. Janet couldn't think straight, she knew he was out there, but she hoped he would just leave her alone. She hadn't gone to the police yet because she thought that it would only make him mad.

Mary B and William were about thirty minutes from home, when all of a sudden, the tire blew out. They were just cruising along and enjoying each other's company, and then out of nowhere there was a loud pop. Good thing they weren't going fast. William pulled over to the side of the road, he was sure he was far enough onto the shoulder. There wasn't any traffic, so he knew he had to change it himself. Mary B being Mary B, asked him if he needed help. He smiled to himself; he knew she could do it. The crazy thing was she was just as good at it as he was, but he would never admit that to her.

William thought to himself, this was the first time he had a blowout in this car the whole time he had it. He was always particular when it came to this car. He was always checking the tires, the oil etc. He only drove the car very little, but he checked the fluids almost daily. Mary B used to tease him that he loved the car more than her. She knew there was no comparison between her and the car, but she knew it got under his skin when she teased.

"You alright in there?" William called out.

"Yes, why wouldn't I be? Are you almost done yet?" William was tightening the last bolt on the tire when a car came through; at that moment it seemed as if he was going a hundred miles per hour.

Before Mary B could turn away the car plowed into William hard enough to take him and the door with it. She realized the car wasn't speeding, she knew that because she was able to catch a glimpse of the license tag. The tag was pretty simple BOV1, at least the part she could recognize. Before her brain caught up with her movement she was out of the car and running to William's side. She held him close and kept reassuring him that he would be okay. He had to be okay. What would Mary B do without him? She couldn't think about that right now, she just sat there with him waiting for someone to drive by. At one point she thought the person driving the car was going to stop but they didn't. The minutes turned into hours before someone finally came. But by that point William had lost so much blood that he had bled out in her arms. Those two hours seemed like an eternity. William and her children were her entire life, what would become of her without him. He was the only man to ever make her heart sing. "God please don't take him from me." There had to be no worse feeling than when you feel the one you love, take their last breath. In that moment Mary B felt like dying herself. She was stronger than she thought.

While William was bleeding out, trouble was headed towards Robert and Davina's home. Trouble was coming in the form of Bo. He was determined to have Janet, and nothing was going to stand in his way. He had already come too far to turn back now. Something that Janet never knew was that Bo had been diagnosed as a sociopath. This diagnosis happened earlier before they had met, but with medication he was able to hide the majority of his symptoms. Part of his diagnosis was that he would get obsessed with people and objects, unfortunately once he became fixated on them, it was over. He became relentless. His behavior had gotten out of control yet again.

Once he saw Janet at the restaurant after all that time, he couldn't make himself just walk away from her. Bo needed to be near her. He was off his meds and he knew he should start taking them again, but for some reason he just couldn't bring himself to do it. He knew what he had done when he hit William with his car. He was jealous, he couldn't help it. Nothing was going to keep him from getting his Janet back.

Bo didn't know that William was Janet's uncle; he just knew that she was riding with him a little too much for his liking. Anyone who was getting a piece of Janet's time was seen a threat. At least that is how Bo saw it. The one thing his father taught him was, if you want something don't let anything or anyone stand in your way. Although his father didn't leave him with too many valuable life lessons, that was the one that stuck with him.

He pulled up to Robert's house, and started blowing his

horn. On the way over he had texted Janet and asked if he could just talk to her. At first Janet said no, but when he kept texting and then he called, she finally agreed. Janet thought that since he already knew where she was at, she didn't want to risk him doing anything to harm her family. She thought it was a smart move. She told Robert what was going on just in case things got a little crazy.

When she went outside, she had her Glock on her. She had almost left it at home, but something reminded her right before she left the house to grab it. She knew enough to protect herself. Janet's heartbeat was racing from the rush of adrenaline, she tried to calm it down, and she couldn't let him know she was scared. "What's up Bo? You wanted to meet with me, so here I am. What can I do for you?"

Bo stepped in closer to close the distance. He reached in for a hug, and Janet stepped quickly back. She was determined to stay out of his reach. "It's going to be like that? Do you remember how it used to be? It wasn't always bad. We did have some good times, right? Come on babe, I came all this way to be with you." He tried to act charmingly, but Janet knew all too well what lurked under that facade.

"Bo, I never asked for you to come find me. I was happy rebuilding my life, I honestly don't know what you want from me?"

The look in Bo's eyes scared her, she tried to look away, but he locked in on her gaze. "Janet, you know that I told you a long time ago that I wasn't going to be without you. I allowed you to do your own thing for these last few years, but I've always been where you were. I have always known where you lived, where you worked. I was good though, because you never knew I was there." Bo saw the look of disbelief spark in her eyes. "Do you remember the guy at Starbucks, he gave you his number? You even called him once, but the next time you went to that Starbucks he no longer worked there. Yeah that was all me. I told you if I couldn't have you no one would."

"If you knew where I was and you did all of that, why didn't I see you?"

With a smug look on his face he replied smoothly, "I didn't want you to. The only reason you see me now is because I allowed it to happen. I got tired of constantly being in the shadows."

Janet couldn't believe what she was hearing but she started reflecting back over the last few years. There were a few times when something reminded her of him. At the time she thought she was just overthinking things. So, she would quickly dismiss the event. "Bo, you know that you have a problem, right?"

"My problem has always been you since the day I laid eyes on you." Bo moved in towards her again, this time he was too quick for her to move away. Before she knew it, his hands were wrapped around her neck.

Robert came running from the house, but he stopped in his tracks. Bo saw him coming for him and tightened his grip. "If you don't stop, I will squeeze the life out of her. So, think about your choices my man. I love her but no one else will ever have her if I can't." Janet felt his hands tightening, and her breathing was shallow, and she was starting to see stars, she knew she was close to losing consciousness. She remembered that she had her gun. She would only have one shot, so she had to make it count. She knew if she didn't hit him hard enough to make him let go, he would surely kill her.

Janet pulled the gun from her sweatshirt pocket and put it to his stomach and pulled the trigger. Robert yelled out for Jean to call 911. Bo, stumbled back, and grabbed his stomach. He looked at his bloody hand and his eyes were wide with shock. He couldn't believe she actually shot him "Why would you shoot me? I never meant to hurt you, all I wanted was to love you Janet, and I wanted you to love me." He fell back onto the ground, the blood flowing from the wound. Robert put a towel over the wound to try and stop the bleeding. Bo knew he was going to have a lot to answer for once the police showed up, so he asked for one favor. "Please call my dad and tell him what happened. Yes, all of it. He will know what to do."

At that moment Janet saw a glimpse of the man she fell in love with. Even though physically he towered over her, at that moment he seemed so small. "Tell me his name and where the number is and then you need to stop talking and save your strength. The ambulance should be here soon." No sooner had she spoke the words; she could hear the sirens approaching in the distance.

Bo was struggling to speak; he barely managed to give her his dad's name. "His number is 555-0555, and his name is Bobby." Within minutes the police had arrived along with the ambulance. Things happened pretty quickly after that. They loaded Bo onto a stretcher and into the ambulance, and he was gone. The police stayed behind to get Janet's statement. She was still understandably shaken up by the whole ordeal.

She found her voice to answer the questions that Officer

Wilson was asking of her. "Tell me what happened ma'am? I need as many details as you can remember that way I won't have to ask again, and hopefully no one else will either."

Davina was by Janet's side, as was Robert, lending her their strength. "The guy that was taken away in the ambulance was my ex. He has tried to take my life on several occasions. Tonight, will hopefully be the last time,"

"Did you file charges on him at any time?" Officer Wilson asked, jotting notes down on a notepad.

Janet took a deep breath, "No I didn't because I thought he was no longer a factor in my life. I was too scared to do that to be honest. I knew that if he found out I had taken legal action and spoke to the police it would only make the situation worse. I was worried his behavior would escalate, and that he would become even more dangerous. He told me today that even though I thought he was no longer a factor, he has been right there the whole time, from the moment I left town. He told me, that he could have gotten to me at any time he wanted to. The only reason why I had noticed him now was because he allowed me to. What kind of foolishness is that? I mean what can you say to something that?"

Officer Wilson asked her, "So what happened here tonight exactly as you remember it?"

Janet was getting frustrated just talking about it. She knew she had to do it either here now, or later down at the station. "I've been here with my family celebrating the New Year, well trying to anyway. Bo had called and texted me earlier. After the first time or two I turned my phone off. He normally doesn't leave a voicemail when he calls but tonight, he did. He told me that he wanted to start over, and that he still loved me. He told me that he knew I sometimes ride with my uncle in his 1967 Shelby. Come to think of it, he didn't know that it was my uncle's car. He thought it was just some guy, and I guess that made him angry. He knew I was here, when I turned my phone back on there was all kinds of escalating messages on my phone. Then he kept texting me, asking to see me. At first, I said no, but he just kept on and then he called asking to just speak with me. I didn't want to endanger my family, so I agreed to meet with him."

"Where did you get the gun? Did you come here with it to intentionally lure Bo here to cause him harm?" Officer Wilson was taking all this in. Janet seemed to be very forthcoming.

"No, No, why would I do something that? I hoped he had left town. I didn't know for sure until I was here that he was still around. We bumped into him awhile back at a restaurant close to home. But I haven't seen him since. I have my gun and a permit to carry it and I have it for protection. Had I not had it, that would have been me you were carting off in the ambulance."

Just then, Officer Wilson received a call across the radio, and so he excused himself for a moment. When he came back, he asked where the Shelby was at now. Janet told him that her aunt and uncle had left a few hours ago to head back home. They should be there by now. Janet asked why he asked.

"The call I just received, was about an accident on the highway about an hour and a half from here. It involved a 1967 Shelby, and there was a fatality. I was just inquiring because you mentioned a car matching that description earlier."

Before Officer Wilson even stopped speaking Robert,

jumped into the conversation, "What kind of accident? Is everyone okay? That is my parents in that car. Please tell me they are okay?" Robert looked at Jean and pulled her to him and held her close as they waited for the officer to speak.

"Sir, the only thing I can tell you for sure is that it wasn't pretty. There was a fatality. I don't know who or all the details of what occurred. There was a hit and run, I was told that they did get the plate number, so hopefully that should help find the person responsible."

Robert nearly lost his mind when the officer said there was a fatality. His heart was beating fast, he couldn't calm down. No matter who it was, he knew his life was going to be irrevocably changed after that night.

Jean couldn't take it, "You said the accident occurred an hour and half away? Are they still on the scene? Where are my parents? Please tell me, I've got to get to them." As much as Robert understood his sister's need to get to them, he held her back. Her eyes were watery, and he knew all too well what that meant. He knew he couldn't allow her to go off like that. Whoever did this was going to pay.

"Settle down ma'am, there is an officer with them now. The woman survived; the man that was with her was struck down." Although Jean and Robert wanted to know who survived, they really didn't. They couldn't believe what they had just heard. Jean's knees buckled underneath her, and she collapsed to the ground. Robert tried to catch her, but he was unsuccessful. He had no choice but to assist her to the ground. He sat down with her and held her and rocked her.

Davina was in shock, she didn't know what to do, or what to say. She knew the family would never be the same. Although William didn't talk a lot, he was a major part of their family. He held them down just as much as Mary B. William was the father she never knew. *Oh, my goodness, what will happen to Mary B?* Davina knew she wasn't fragile but losing the love of your life, would cause even Superwoman to break. And Mary B was just that, she was their Superwoman.

CHAPTER THREE

AT THAT MOMENT DAVINA WAS STANDING AT THE BACK of Bo's car. The officer walked past her, and she touched his arm to get his attention. "Yes ma'am, can I help you?" Davina had noticed that the front of Bo's car had some damage to it. Enough damage to have possibly been in a recent accident. She prayed that she was wrong, but she wanted the officer to check the tag and verify if it was the same. She hated seeing her husband and his sister torn up like they were. But everyone deserved to know the whole truth. Officer Wilson asked for the plate number of the vehicle identified in the hit and run.

Mary B was all too eager to tell the officer that was with her. "BOV1," she said, fearing she might not remember it if she didn't speak up right then. Davina could hear her yelling into the walkie. "Do you know who did this to my husband?"

"Miss, please calm down, we are following up on a lead. Hopefully we will know something soon. I was asked to see if you wanted to go back to your son's home or to your house?" Officer Johnson knew this woman needed her family even if she didn't realize it.

"If this is about what I would like to do, I'd like to have my husband standing here beside me instead of you. I pray you don't take that the wrong way. I would like to go back to where my family is. On second thought I need to go home. I need time to process this and make all the necessary arrangements." Mary B was struggling to hold back the tears. No matter what was thrown her way, she vowed that she would not wear her feelings on her sleeve, no matter what.

"No offense taken ma'am. You deserve to be angry or out of sorts, you have just suffered a horrific tragedy. Are you sure you don't want to go to the hospital? I know the EMS tech checked you out, but I would feel better if you went and were fully checked out."

"No, I'm fine; I'm not going to any hospital. I just want to go home. Can you take me home please?"

"Yes ma'am, I can do that. I just need to let the other officer know that I'm going to drop you home, so they won't be looking for me. I also need to let the other officer who inquired about the license tag know that you are going home in case there are any other questions." Mary B nodded her head and walked towards the police car.

When Officer Wilson heard the tag that the other officer read out, he looked immediately to Davina. She was shaking her head and trying to understand, just what had happened. She knew the only one who could tell her that was Bo.

Officer Wilson tried to make Davina feel a little better. He told her at least they had the guy who killed her father in law in custody. He assured her that they would put officers on him around the clock while he was in the hospital.

Wilson called for the forensic team and a tow truck to take Bo's car to get impounded once the crime scene techs had removed any evidence, they might need from it to form a case.

Davina still wasn't feeling well about having to tell Robert or Jean, that it was Bo who ran over their daddy. She looked over at Janet who was in just as much in shock as everyone else at this point. How would she recover from this? Shooting someone can't be easy. Davina went to her; she needed to tell her the truth before someone else did. Truth was Davina didn't know how Robert and Jean would act once they found out, and she didn't know how Janet would react either. Davina wondered how much more tragedy this family could endure. God himself was the only one who knew the answer to that. Davina hugged Janet and asked her how she was holding up. The paramedics had done a preliminary check of her and told her she should be okay.

Janet told Davina physically she was okay. "Body wise Davina, I'm okay, mentally and emotionally I just don't know. I should have left when I started to. None of this would have happened if I did. Thank God the children remained asleep throughout this whole thing. I would never forgive myself if they were involved with this."

"This isn't your fault Janet. We all were excited to have you as a part of this family, and not a single one of us regretted that you stayed."

"Yeah nobody regretted it until now. This is horrible, I almost killed a man tonight. Yes, I was defending myself, but that doesn't change the fact that I almost killed him. He wasn't always horrible; he was a loving man." Janet dragged her hands down her face and sighed, it felt like the world was spinning way too fast, and she had no way of keeping up.

Davina felt that she had to tell her now, so maybe she wouldn't feel so bad and be so hard on herself. "Janet, umm listen, I've got something I've got to tell you and it won't be easy to hear, but just know sometimes things happen for a reason." Janet looked confused. "The thing is Bo was driving the car that struck William." Davina could see Janet's eyes widen in disbelief. "The license plate matches the one Mary B saw driving away."

Janet was shaking her head, no. "That cant... that can't possibly be true. He would do whatever to me but to someone else? That is just crazy." At that moment she remembered the conversation that she and Bo had. Oh my God, he had told her he had seen her getting in and out of that car. What if he really thought William and she were together? As crazy as it sounded, her knowing Bo as she did, it began to make sense.

Janet couldn't believe what was happening. Her ex killed her uncle and she almost killed her ex. In the blink of an eye she had brought so much pain upon this family, her family. They would never forgive her. She didn't think she would ever forgive herself. Janet wished that she had killed him, at least that would have been the end of him; he would never be able to hurt anyone else. She could have given the family that comfort at least. Looking over at Robert and Jean she felt an overwhelming sadness descend upon her like a heavy velvet cloak.

Tim, who had been moving back and forth from the house to check on the children and back out to the front lawn to check on his wife, couldn't believe what was going on. He heard the officer say that Mary B wanted to go home. So, he called Christian and asked if he could just meet her there. Tim didn't want to go into the details over the phone and he told his dad he probably wouldn't believe him if he did. Christian agreed to get to her as soon as possible.

He had stayed in town instead of driving to Robert's that night and went to a New Year Eve party with some of his co-workers instead. He felt like the family needed some time to bond. He didn't want to feel like a third wheel. Christian ended up connecting with an old friend and they went back to her place for conversation and drinks, neither wanted the night to end just yet. It wasn't too long before Tim called, and the date was cut short anyway. Christian promised they would see each other soon. Christian apologized, but he said it was a family emergency. Sasha said she understood and that there was no need to apologize. She gave him her number and kissed him on the cheek. Christian smiled and left; he didn't know what was going on, but it had to be serious.

He noticed that Tim had mentioned that Mary B was going home. His mind wandered what about William? Christian knew all too well that unless he was just hanging out with Christian that Mary B wasn't too far from William's side. He figured maybe William stayed back to help out with something, and they just wanted to make sure Mary B was okay. Either way he was happy to do it. This family took him in, even though it was a complicated reason he became part of the family. Nothing could have prepared him for the truth.

When Christian arrived at Mary B's, a police car was there. The officer was escorting her to the door. "I'm fine, you can go officer. I just want to be alone right now. Thank you for everything. I hope you find the man responsible."

"Are you sure that you don't want me to come in and just check the house ma'am to make sure everything is okay?" Mary B nodded as she fumbled in her purse trying to find her keys. Just then Christian walked up; he told the officer that he would take it from there. The officer looked at Mary B to make sure she was okay with this guy who seemed to come from out of nowhere. Again, Mary B nodded. Christian reached for her keys so that he could unlock the door. She gave them to him without hesitation. The officer headed back to her car. "Take care ma'am," she said as Mary B was walking in the door.

Once inside Mary B looked at Christian, "What are you doing here? Weren't you out celebrating this New Year?"

"I was, but I got a call that I needed to be here, so here I am. I can tell from the look in your eyes that something is very wrong. What is it?" Mary B let out a deep breath and began to tell him what happened. Her voice was shaking, and tears started to descend. Christian listened intently to her words. She told him that they had left Robert and Davina's to head home, all was well until they got a flat tire. She relived the moments leading up to William's death. Christian was to learn later that this was only a small part of that day's events that would forever change them all. Christian asked if it was okay if he stayed with her at least until the kids returned. She told him it was fine, as long as he didn't make a fuss over her. He could only smile, because in truth he knew she was the strong one, but even those of us that are strong need to lean on others at times. He agreed but told her to please go and lay down at least for a bit.

Surprisingly she didn't argue, and she went to her room to do just that. There she stayed until early that afternoon when she came out in a frantic uproar. Mary B asked if he could drive her to the accident scene. At first, Christian was a little hesitant. So, Mary B explained she needed to see if she could find his ring. She remembered it wasn't on his finger when they took his body, so that meant it was out there somewhere. Christian drove her out there. Before she could get out of the car, she broke down in tears. "I'm so sorry Christian, I should not have asked you to drive me here. I'm not ready to face it yet, I thought I could if I just stay focused on his ring, but I can't, I'm not strong enough."

"Mary B, you are one of the strongest people I know. But even you have to take a break and take the S off your chest for a moment. I know you've had to be the strong one for your family. But please let them and let me help you now. You know I loved William, he accepted me with flaws and all, and we became like brothers. So, let me repay his kindness by being here for the love of his life." He saw a small smile, but a smile, nonetheless, come across her face. "Yes, the love of his life. He told me that on so many occasions, I thought you had programmed him to say it." She smiled again, as her gaze turned outside.

"I will try and look for the ring, since we are here. That is unless you are ready to go, and if that is the case, I will take you home or wherever you want to go." She grabbed his hand and told him thank you. She also told him that if he didn't mind looking for it, she would be forever grateful.

CHAPTER FOUR

JEAN AND TIM HEADED FOR HOME WITH THE CHILDREN.
Jean hadn't spoken with her mom, when she had called
Mary B didn't answer. Jean didn't want to push her mom too
hard, too soon, so she said she would wait and talk to her in
person. Besides she wasn't sure just what all her mom knew
at that point, if anything, about what had happened at
Robert's after she and William had left.

Tim told Jean that he would take the kids home and get
them settled and then come back to get her later, unless she
wanted or needed him with her now. Jean told him she
wanted some time alone with her mom, but that she would
call him when she was ready to come home. Tim agreed only
after she promised she would call him if she changed her
mind and needed him over there sooner.

When Jean arrived at Mary B's, she was in the kitchen
cooking dinner. Jean walked in and kissed her mom on the
cheek. "Hey Momma, I want to ask how you are doing but I
know you won't give me the honest answer." Mary B looked

at Jean and gave her a half smile. "What are you cooking? It smells like my favorites."

"Depends on what your favorites are. I seem to recall you like baked chicken, baked macaroni and cheese, cabbage and of course homemade biscuits. So, if that is what you would call some of your favorites, then I guess you would be correct." Mary B always had a slick sense of humor and Jean knew that would never change.

"Mom, you know that you know what my favorites are. You made them my favorites from the time I was small. That was one of the things I missed when I was gone. The scraps that I had to survive on were horrible." Jean knew that Mary B didn't like talking about the time she was gone, but if it kept her mind off the recent events then it was worth it.

Although Jean knew she would have to get her mom to start talking about it sooner rather than later. She knew it to be true, when Mary B set a place for William at the head of the table. Mary B told her to sit down, so that Daddy could say the blessing. Jean wasn't sure what to say to her mom. "Momma, you know Daddy isn't there tonight right?"

Mary looked at Jean with an undecipherable look and simply said, "He will always be here. He is the man of my house and he will always sit at the head of my table. I understand what you're saying child, but I honestly don't know how to be without him. I'm not crazy, I know he is not there physically, but my mind won't release him just yet."

Jean's heart melted; she didn't know how to help her mom at that moment. She herself was trying to stay strong and deal with the fact that her daddy wouldn't be there to hug her and tell her everything was going to be alright any longer. William always knew what to say and when to say it. She couldn't remember a time when he had even so much as raised his voice at her or Robert. He was able to get his point across without the drama. If looks could make you straighten up and act right, he had that power.

A lot of people always thought that it was Mary B who ran the house. The funny thing was she didn't make a move unless William agreed on it, he was fine with letting her be the enforcer of the family. Looking around the house now, there was so much of her father even in the kitchen. The shelves he had built in the pantry to give Mary B that extra space she said she just had to have. In the hallway that led to the living room where all of their family pictures were meticulously hung. Her dad was always smiling. That is how she would remember him.

Jean snapped back to the present, she was supposed to be helping her mom to deal with the harsh reality of not having her husband there with her anymore. Mary B had gotten up from the table, her plate untouched; she couldn't bring herself to eat. It didn't seem right to be eating without William. She walked over to where William's favorite chair was and just sank down into it. Before she could stop it the tears came. It was if the floodgates had been raised and the maelstrom of emotions had been unleashed.

Mary B hadn't really cried for her husband until now, sure she shed tears when it happened, but she was holding back because she didn't want William to see her in that way. That would have eaten him up as he made his journey into the afterlife. He hated seeing his wife cry, so she could not let his last vision of her be that of her being sad. Jean realized that she couldn't do this on her own. She called Robert for backup; she was going to need his help to tell Mary B the rest of the story. Jean thought it would be better to do it now rather than waiting.

Janet attempted to dial the number Bo had given her several times, but she could never complete it. She needed to see him, because she needed to know why. There had to be a real reason for him to kill William. That was going to be something she had to live with for the rest of her life. She wanted to go to the hospital, but she didn't want to go alone. Janet knew the cops would be there, but she was still scared to be alone in the same room with him. She couldn't trust that she wouldn't try and end his life. After she saw him, she would call his dad. No matter what he had done and what had gotten them to this point a small part of her still loved him. She hated herself because of that.

Bo had done nothing except to cause her heartache and attempt to kill her on more than one occasion. He changed the landscape of her family forever. Bo took a part of her that would never be replaced. William was the father she wished she had while growing up, she finally had him in her life, and just like that he was gone.

"Vina, can you do me a favor? You can say no if you want and I will understand, but I need to go to the hospital. I need to see Bo, I need closure. So, what I'm asking is; would you go with me? You don't have to go into the room if you don't want to." Janet asked, staring down at her hands, not wanting to meet Davina's gaze.

Davina was hesitant at first, but she knew if Janet was asking, then it was important. She agreed to go with her. Davina told Robert where they were going just in case something happened. Robert told her that he was heading home to go see Jean and his mom. Davina asked him, if he needed her to be there, but he said that he could manage and that she could join him once they knew more about when the arrangements would take place.

Robert told her that Jean was having a hard time dealing with William being gone, and that was making it hard to be there for Mary B. "Jean thinks it is better to go ahead and tell Momma everything. That way she can digest it and move on, instead of it coming back to haunt her later." Robert thought it was a good idea for her to go with Janet; she didn't need to be alone. Janet was taking everything that happened personally. They tried to assure her that it wasn't her fault. That wasn't good enough for her. She didn't think she would ever forgive herself, or at least that's what she told Robert a few times.

Janet and Davina arrived at the hospital and were escorted to Bo's room. Officer Wilson had arranged for her to be able to talk to him. Janet wasn't expecting to see him hooked up to several machines. He had lost a lot of blood that night. The bullet had pierced his right lung, so for now he was getting assistance with his breathing. Janet never wanted to kill him; she only wanted to make him let her go.

Bo turned to face her, when she walked in. "You came to see me; I knew you still loved me. Did you call my pops?"

"I didn't come because I love you. I came because I need answers and I need to understand. Why did you kill my uncle? You remember the story I told you of my family. You know the one where I was all alone. Is any of this ringing a bell? Well it just so happens that I am no longer alone. I do have family and I was enjoying getting to know them until you came along. It was by chance that I met them. But now you've ruined that for me. How can I expect them to ever forgive me?" Janet said tearfully.

It was a minute before Bo could speak. "Janet, baby I'm sorry. I didn't mean to kill him, it just sort of happened, I was angry with you. You weren't returning my calls and I kept seeing you with him."

"I was with them all! The only reason I was with him more is because he was trying to protect me from you and your craziness."

"I didn't know that Janet. I just knew you weren't with me. I've missed you. I tried to stay away and let you live your life, but it just got hard for me. There is something that you never knew about me. I've got some issues I'm dealing with, I'm supposed to take medication, but I stopped taking them. I thought I could get you back, so I didn't feel like I needed them anymore. I was wrong. Please say that you called my dad."

Janet shook her head no. "I tried to call but I never completed it. I will call him when I leave here." Just then there was a knock at the door, a man walked in. Bo's eyes got big, "Dad, how did you know where I was?"

"I told you a long time ago son, that I know everything when it comes to mine. What are you doing in this town? I left this place in the wind a long time ago, and never looked back. Yet here I am back where I started. What's going on?" Bobby knew all too well that this town could do to a person.

"Dad, this is Janet, she is the one I told you about a few years ago." Bo said, gesturing over to where Janet was standing.

Until that moment he hadn't paid much attention to her.

"Yes, the one who had your nose open. So, open you were doing all kinds of crazy things. I thought I told you to leave her alone."

Bo shook his head affirmatively. "Yeah you told me to leave her alone and I tried to, but I couldn't. Dad, I've done something terrible. I killed someone."

"You did what? What were you thinking? How stupid could you be? I guess you're expecting for me to pull you out of the fire again this time. I won't always be around to save your sorry behind. I'll be back later. I need to get my attorney down here before you get questioned too much. I should have never come back here, all this town means is a lot of bad memories, and you are making it worse. For the love of God don't open your mouth until I get back. If anyone asks any questions keep your mouth closed. Do you understand me?" In a flash he was out the door. He didn't wait for an answer.

Bo looked at Janet; he looked like a little boy that had been just scolded by his father. She actually felt sorry for him. "Janet, that is my father, Bobby. I know you probably think that I'm just as worthless as he does. I know it doesn't make anything better, but I am truly sorry for what happened to your uncle. I pray that one day you will be able to forgive me." With that Janet decided that it was time for her to go. She got answers but she realized they didn't help in the grand scheme of things. William was still gone, and it didn't make things go back to normal as she had hoped.

Before she could get out of the door good, Davina was asking her, "Who was that man?" Janet looked puzzled at first but answered her. "That was Bobby, Bo's father. Why? What's going on?"

Davina was almost sure that the man she saw rushing

into and out of that room was her father. But she needed to be sure before she said anything. She didn't want to mention it and it wasn't true. "I was just wondering because he was moving so fast. So, did you find out what you wanted to know? Were you tempted to put the pillow over his face and smother him?"

Janet smiled. "No, I didn't want to smother him. I actually feel sorry for him. He told me he has some issues. Mental ones and he was off his medication. I didn't realize that he was on any while we were together. He was good at hiding that fact. His dad just went in on him. He completely disregarded the fact that I was still standing there."

When they arrived home, Davina went to go look for the picture that she had of her mom and her biological father. She was getting frustrated, because at first, she was having a problem finding it. She took a few deep breaths and started her search again. Within moments she had found the picture. "Janet! Janet! I need you to look at something for me. I need to see if you see what I see."

Davina was being extra cryptic, and Janet didn't understand why. As soon as she saw the picture that Davina had in her hand, she knew why. Even from a distance she could tell there was a resemblance to the man she had just seen today. "What is that? Who is that?"

Davina said, "That is my dad. I never really knew him. All I gather from this picture is that he seemed to have been happy about me when I was in my mom's tummy, but he didn't stick around long after I was born. If he is in fact the man at the hospital, I'm not sure that I want to bother him with any of this. He didn't seem to be very approachable." Davina had kept that part of her life to herself. She always acted as if not knowing her father didn't matter. Deep down she had to admit that it did. How could someone walk away from their own flesh and blood? What did that say about him or about the child that was left behind?

"Davina that does look like it could be Bo's father, just a younger version. I could take that picture to Bo and ask him if he thinks it could be him." Janet said helpfully as she passed the photograph back over to Davina.

Davina wasn't sure if that was a good idea. If this was true, then she had a brother who tried to kill her friend and who had managed to kill her husband's father. So much was going on and too quickly. How can she go from disliking this guy who was the cause of a lot of pain that was just starting, to be his sister? What if they didn't want to know who she was? Clearly, they weren't looking for her. Bobby knew there was a child that he left behind, but not once even after her mom passed did he try to find her. "I need to talk to Robert about all of this. He may want me to leave well enough alone. My mind is all over the place right now."

If anyone should understand how she was feeling it would be Janet. "Davina you know I just found my family and I am thankful every day for you guys. If you and Bo are related it may not have started off the way we would have wanted it to, but sometimes God works in different ways. We have to trust him and that for everything there is a purpose. It may be for nothing more than to remind us where we come from, so you won't have that emptiness in your heart. It can be scary to find out. I was terrified, but because of William, I now have you all. We could always check his blood against yours. That way no one would know except you, you know our family has a lot of people in the medical field. We can get a sample for the test with no problem." Janet tried to lighten the mood. She could see the stress shimmering in Davina's eyes. Finally, Davina allowed a smile to make its way onto her face. *One step at a time,* Janet thought to herself.

CHAPTER FIVE

CHRISTIAN HAD BEEN MAINTAINING HIS POST IN watching over Mary B. He was there most nights for supper, and then he would go home and do it all again the next day. Sasha was staying close to Christian's heels. He didn't like the clinginess, but he tolerated it because he was lonely. Christian found that he could talk to Mary B freely, and she offered up advice that made sense.

She told him to watch out; it seemed as if Sasha was looking for something serious, and possibly a payday. He explained that she was in the medical field, so he didn't think that was the case. "Christian you are a good man. I see why my William took to you, but when it comes to women you are just as naïve as you want to be. That woman has targeted you. Mark my words, if you don't believe me, stand her up a time or two and see what happens. I'm almost certain she wonders why you are over here with me most nights for dinner. Then again you can invite her over here; I still know how to make them jealous." Mary B and Christian both laughed a good laugh.

It had been awhile since Mary B had allowed herself to laugh. Everything with William was still fresh. "Christian I meant to ask you something. I know that I have been holding onto William's body for almost two weeks now, but I have to find his ring. I know you have taken me out there a few times already. I will understand if you don't want to." Mary B started to say before Christian waved his hand in the air, effectively halting any further talk on the subject.

"That is absolute nonsense. I will help you look for the ring. I remember him telling me the story of that ring, it was near and dear to him. He knew who it was meant for, and he kept it and himself for you."

Mary B blushed because she knew the story all too well. "Thank you for everything you have done for me Christian. As for your lady friend, spend time with her and stop worrying about me. Do it with a fresh set of eyes though, that way you can see what she is all about. If she is right for you, you will know it. Don't be a fool; sometimes being alone is not the worst thing that could happen. Besides as long as you are a part of this family you will never be alone."

Christian nodded his head in agreement. "So, if I'm not here for dinner a few nights, you will be okay?" Mary B nodded back.

BOBBY MADE IT BACK TO THE HOSPITAL TO SEE BO. HE couldn't shake the feeling that he knew the young girl that was outside of his son's room. Even though he only had a brief glimpse there was something familiar about her. "Bo, how are you feeling son? I've spoken with my attorney and they will be here in a few days. Make sure you keep your mouth closed until he arrives."

"Dad, I did those things and whatever has to happen, I'm okay with it. I took a life; I was out of control." Tears filled Bo's eyes.

"Yes, you did it, but you were without your medications. That will play a role in your defense. We can even go after Janet, I know you still have feelings for her, but my God son, she tried to kill you."

"She had every right to do that. To be honest I wish she would have killed me. I thought she had, and I was at peace with things. I put that woman through all kinds of hell, and she loved me through it all. Looking back Dad, I attempted to kill her on several occasions, and all I offered up was a half apology and a sorry, I love you. She kept telling me that isn't what love does. I would only hit her more, I wanted to make sure that no one else wanted her. She meant so much to me, and I should have given her the world, instead I tore hers apart. I don't deserve to live. So, I take full responsibility for all of it, I refuse to press charges against her. Looking at your face Dad, I know that I've disappointed you, but I've disappointed myself even more."

Bobby couldn't deny how proud he was of his son at that moment. He realized his son was more of a man than he had been. His son came by it honestly, the way he treated women. Bobby had been horrible to the women in his past. There were things he wished he could tell his son, but he couldn't bear the thought that he would think less of him.

When he was younger, he was dumb and stupid, just like a lot of boys that age. He and his friends took things to a whole different level. Bo would understand that his dad had sold drugs, but Bobby didn't think he could forgive the fact that he kidnapped women and pimped some out. Bobby hated that part of his past. He tried to rectify it when his life was spared, and he ran and didn't look back.

Bobby had vowed never to hurt women in that way or any way if he could help it. When he found out that he was having a boy, his life changed. There wasn't a day that went by that he didn't think about the little girl he left behind. He was so caught up in that world; he didn't trust himself around her. What if he did that to his daughter or if someone else did in retaliation for something he did? He would have definitely caught a murder charge. Bobby often wondered what happened to her, and he prayed that she was okay.

Bobby wanted to track his child down, but he didn't want to stir that pot. What would he say to her if he had found her? This town brought so many memories back to him, and they were not good ones. Well there was a good one, and that was when he conceived his little girl. How could he ever bring himself to tell his son the truth?

"Dad, are you okay?" Bobby looked as if he was a thousand miles away. "I am sorry Dad, and I know sorry doesn't fix anything. I need to get some help, that man didn't deserve to die, and I just left him there. He bled out in front of his wife, and there is nothing good or honorable about that. That's the last memory she will have of him, and that is something I will live with for the rest of my life. It doesn't stop me from loving Janet, but I have to let her go. It's kind of late, but I realize that it's not healthy this path I was on."

Bobby's eyes teared up, "Son, even though this situation isn't ideal. I want you to know that I am proud of you, and the fact that you want to handle it like a man. I am only upset because it's your life, and it will never be the same. There are some things that I will tell you about your father one day, and then maybe you will understand why everything you are going through affects me so much."

LATER THAT NIGHT WHEN ROBERT CAME HOME, HE SAW Davina sitting in the middle of the floor looking at a picture, it was one he didn't recognize. "Babe, what's going on? Why are you sitting here in the middle of the floor? What is that, that you are looking at?" Robert rattled off a hundred questions, and Davina offered no reply it was like she was in a daze. "Babe?" Robert shakes his wife, and she nearly jumps out of her skin.

"Robert, hey, what are you doing home? I thought you were staying with your mom for a few days. The babies and I are okay." Davina looked up at him, like she was surprised he was standing there in front of her.

"Funny Vina, but you don't look okay. Why don't you tell me what's going on? Who is that in the picture and why are you sitting here like this?" Robert asked with a confused expression on his face.

Davina didn't know where to begin, she knew it must have looked strange with her just sitting there in the dark, well almost dark with pictures scattered all over the floor. She wasn't sure she could tell him just yet, there may not be anything to tell. Looking into Robert's eyes she knew he wouldn't stop until she told him something. "It's just a picture of my mom and dad, at least who I've always believed him to be. I stumbled across the picture, and with all that has happened with William, it made me long for her." She looked at Robert to see if he was buying her story, it was partially true.

"Yeah losing my dad has been a hard thing to swallow. I remember Janet saying something about going to see Bo at the hospital. Did she go? Did you go with her?" Robert asked in disgust, "Is the punk still alive, or did Janet kill him?"

It was at that moment that Davina knew she had to be honest with Robert, no matter if it was true or not. "Yeah, I went with her, and he is still alive. He should make a full recovery, it won't be an easy process, but he should be fine. Actually, going to see him is what prompted me to look for this picture." Robert looked at her quizzically, not sure where she was heading with this. "While I was waiting outside, so that Janet could get some answers from him, this guy who looks an awful lot like the man in this picture here, went to see Bo. I later learned that the guy is Bo's dad."

Robert went from confused to almost livid, "Vina so what are you saying? Are you telling me that you may be related to this man who killed my father in cold blood?" Davina wished that she could take the conversation back. she didn't think it was such a good idea to be honest with him all of a sudden. She had only seen Robert angry a few times in their life together and it never ended well.

"Robert, I don't know. I just know that he looks an awful lot like this picture. He didn't look at me like he knew who I was so I could be wrong. I'd rather be wrong actually. Do you have any idea how it makes me feel to know that someone who is possibly my brother killed William? He was like my father. Not once did he ever judge me from my background. Babe say something?"

"What do you want me to say Vina? That I'm happy you found your dad. Do you remember that man left your mom? Do you remember that he pimped her out like a piece of meat? The worst and best thing he did was leaving you behind, because you didn't have to grow up with a piece of scum like him. I know you try and act like not having or knowing your biological dad didn't matter, but I know the truth. I know you feel like you missed out on that part of life."

Now Davina was tearing up, "Babe, yes I felt like I was missing something. I'm thankful for being blessed with Joshua as my dad. He showed me in so many ways that I was wanted. And he didn't have to do any of the things he did, but he did and never asked for anything in return. He did one heck of a job with me; without him I may have ended up just like my mom." Davina wanted to end the conversation there, but she knew he wasn't going to let it rest. She tried to tell him; she didn't care if the guy in the picture was the same that she had seen that day.

But Robert wasn't going for it. "So, Vina, what are you going to do? Are you going to confront this guy? If you are then I need to be there." That was just it though, Davina hadn't planned on bringing it up, at least not yet.

LATER THAT EVENING BOBBY kept thinking about the woman he had seen. He tried his best not to stare at her. Something was familiar about her, but he dismissed it and told himself it couldn't be her. She was born in a town a few hours away; a town he swore he would never go back to. His life, and his freedom depended on him staying away from there. Bobby had done well up until now, when he left, he never looked back.

Bobby was given a second chance and he made good on it. When he left town, he cleaned himself up, if one didn't know you would have thought the man he was now, and the one he had been, were two totally different people. He hadn't gotten so much as a parking ticket in all those years. But here he was risking it all to be by his son's side.

Bo was only a few years younger than his daughter. It was something about having a boy that made him stay straight, he swore he would give him a good example to follow. He wasn't a saint by any means, he still slipped up with his temper from time to time, and he had put his hands-on Bo's mom a time or two. Each time that it happened he swore it would be the last, eventually he got some help and it was the last time.

Thinking about his little girl, he started having flash-backs of what he had done prior to her birth and after she was born. In his day he was sort of a big deal. If you wanted drugs, he had them, you wanted women, he had them too. Whatever you wanted he could get it. The bad thing about it was that whatever he got, he also used. The one thing they always tell you, is to never use your own product. He didn't get that memo. Bobby shot up and snorted with the best of them. Pretty soon he slipped from reality, he decided that he would kidnap him a few young girls and make some quick money. It was moments like that he wasn't thinking of his daughter, he was long gone from her life at that point, had he been thinking of her surely, he wouldn't have done the things he did. Looking back in retrospect, he shouldn't have done those things. He hurt a lot of people.

Bobby thought about the teenage girl that he had kept locked up, it had been forever since she crossed his thoughts. She was around the same age as his own daughter. The memories of his actions now disgusted him. And he often wondered what happened to her. Bobby knew she was saved because of the bust, but he didn't know how all of that affected her. Until now, he never really worried about running into her or there being a chance that she would recognize him. He had no choice; he had to be here for his son. Bobby planned to stay out of sight as much as possible.

CHAPTER SIX

FINALLY, ON THEIR SEVENTH TRIP TO THE CRASH SITE, they found William's ring. Mary B was holding up burying him until she found it, and she knew the children were getting a little frustrated with her regarding that ring, but she was standing her ground. Earlier that week Jean tried convincing her mom to move on. "Momma, how long are you going to keep Daddy waiting? You know he never liked the cold."

Mary B couldn't help but smile. "I'm not sending him off until I have that ring, and that is that." She said resolutely, and Jean crossed her arms and just observed her mother.

"But Momma you not even burying it with him, are you?"

Mary B started getting frustrated with her daughter. "It does not matter if I'm burying it with him or not. If I bury him and he nor I have it, he will never forgive me. And that is something I will not risk."

Jean knew her mom well enough to know when she was not going to be budged on a matter, and this was one of those times. "Momma you know it's been storming for the last few days, right? That stuff has been blown all around. You can't keep Dad out forever; you wouldn't do that would you?" Mary B didn't answer right away, Jean knew very well that if her mom wanted to, she would keep him in the freezer for as long as it took.

Thankfully they didn't have to wait much longer now. Jean wasn't in a rush to bury her father by any means, he had been her biggest supporter. She had always been Daddy's girl, through all of the bad that happened he never judged her, and she knew he wouldn't. She was thankful to have him set the example of what a man should do and how he should treat those he loved. Jean was having a hard time dealing with the fact he would never be there to hug her or come to her rescue. Mary B knew that both of her children were struggling to find their way without their strong, silent father. She really didn't mean to drag it out, but she had to have the ring.

Emotions were still running high for everyone. Mary B hadn't taken it well when Jean and Robert told her about the fact that it was Bo, Janet's ex who had killed William. One part of her was angry, when Janet wanted to leave, she was the main one talking her into staying. If she would have simply let Janet go, then it would have possibly been Janet lying dead somewhere all alone. So as much as she wanted to hate him, she knew that wasn't going to help anything or change matters any.

Robert told his mom that Janet did shoot, and almost killed him. That wasn't of any consolation to Mary B though. She was happy that Janet had finally stood up for herself, she faced that fear and overcame it. Mary B was happy that she didn't kill him though, because that would have forever weighed on her soul, and that was no way to live. Mary B carried a similar burden. Thinking back that was the one thing William didn't know about her, no one did.

Since Mary B found the ring, she began planning the home going services for her beloved husband. The service was held two weeks after his death. This was the first time that the family had all been together since that horrible morning. Mary B was happy to be around the family, although it didn't feel the same, there seemed to be a massive hole in the canvas of their family.

Kaloni slipped up and asked where Papa was? Davina tried to get her to hush but it was too late. Mary B just smiled and said, "He is in heaven little one. He will forever watch over all of you and keep you safe." At that Kaloni smiled too.

Janet sat behind the pew that housed Mary B, Jean, Tim, Robert, and Davina. She wasn't quite ready to face Mary B just yet. Janet still felt that everything was all her fault, Janet knew that Mary B was a forgiving woman, but she also knew how much she loved William. She knew their love was like none other, and now because of her that was gone.

The service itself was beautiful, Robert and Jean both talked about their dad, and they reminisced over the good times and some of the bad times. The one thing that they couldn't agree on enough was that no matter what their father was always there. He never judged them, not once, even when they did something absolutely crazy. William never judged Jean through all of the drugs and even when she ran away. He just held her in his arms and told her it would be okay. Robert had a bout with drugs and the same thing. William was always there to be supportive, even when he had every right to say I told you so.

Miles wanted to say a little something about his Poppa. "Hi, my name is Miles, and I just want to take a moment of your time. I know that my Poppa would not want us to be sad. Even though the occasion isn't a good one, he would want us to enjoy being together as a family. That was the one thing Poppa always said, I remember that he would always tell me that family above all else. I for one will always try and carry on his wishes. And the best way that we can honor him is to never lose sight of just how much our family means to us." There was not a dry eye in the church when he finished.

Mary B was walking a little slower than normal, but she made her way to the microphone to close out the service. "I don't know how to follow behind my Angel Miles. Since the day he came into our lives he has been a blessing. When I look at him, I see my William. Don't worry Jean, I see you too, but I see my William because they spent so much time together. I can see that he rubbed off on him. That's my William, always thinking ahead. I didn't realize it until this very moment that he left me with a few gifts to always know he is with me. The first was our children, Robert and Jean. And then he left me a mini version of himself in Miles. Lastly, he blessed me with an extension of family, you see, without him, I wouldn't know that I had a sister, and that she had a child, who I am blessed to have here with us today. Even though our family has been through it, William showed us that we are so much stronger together. And so, for my William and for us, that's how we will be, together for always. I love you all."

Christian went up to walk Mary B back to her seat, she

was thankful for this man. When she sat down, she leaned in and whispered to him, that she wanted to go home. Christian leaned over and asked what about going to the burial site. "I've paid my respects and I've given him my love for all eternity, but now I'm about to give out. I just want to rest; would you mind taking me home? If you prefer not, I will get someone to do it."

Christian told her that of course he would take her, and when they were exiting the church to head to the burial site, Mary B got into Christian's car instead. Christian explained to Robert and Jean that he was taking her home. "She seems to be a little weak, she said she was exhausted. I think this has been a little too much for her, so I'll take her so she can rest. I will stay with her this evening and for as long as she needs me to."

"Christian, thank you. We appreciate it so much, are you sure that you don't mind?" Jean was relieved that Christian was there for her mom.

Christian nodded, "You guys go ahead and take care of this, I have her. If she feels like she needs to go to a doctor or needs anything else I will let you know."

Jean was concerned for her mom, but she knew that if she didn't see her father laid to rest, she would regret it. Christian promised that she was in good hands. She assured him that she would be there as soon as she could. Jean knew she couldn't lose her mom also.

Janet realized that Mary B didn't go to the burial site. *That was a bit odd,* she thought. She decided she would stop by Mary B's to make sure she was okay after the service concluded. Besides she had to face her at some point, so she might as well get it over with. She remembered what Mary B had said at church, and thought maybe just maybe, she would forgive her.

When she arrived at Mary B's, she knocked, and Mary B told her to come on in. Janet noticed that Christian had fallen asleep on the couch. "Come on in child, I haven't seen you for a bit. Is everything okay? You're looking like you're scared to talk to me." Janet realized she was being a little hesitant. She locked eyes with Mary B, and she started crying.

"What is going on?" Mary B asked, concern clearly written on her face.

"I'm so sorry for everything. It's my entire fault; if I had just left town none of this would have happened. I know they told you by now that it was Bo, my ex who did that to William. You will never know how much I hate that this happened. William took me in with no hesitation; he made me feel welcome and loved, actually you all did, and that is something that I will always be grateful for and never want to lose."

Mary B was just looking at her and then out the window and back to her again. "Child, weren't you in the church today? Did you not hear what I said? What my Miles said? Family above all else always and without question. You had no control over what Bo or anyone else does. You are exactly where you belong. God makes no mistakes, and yes, he does take Angels to walk with him in his paradise. Sometimes he leaves them here for us to love for a while, and that is the case with William. What most don't know is that he had been a little sick for quite some time now. He made me promise to not tell the family, he didn't want anyone to worry about him. He believed in living life to its fullest.

There will always be obstacles, you can either live your days always wondering and worrying or live it like it's your last. Lord knows we have had some amazing years together. William wouldn't want me to be upset because of how he left us, and he definitely wouldn't want any of us to blame you. So, child understand that we are family for life, you won't get rid of us as easily as that."

Mary B stretched her arms out to Janet and welcomed her into her embrace. When you received a Mary B's hug it felt like all was right with the world.

At that moment Janet felt at peace, the last few weeks have weighed on her heavily. She was torn; she still loved Bo and didn't want to see him hurt. It bothered her that she had actually caused him to almost lose his life. The confusing part was that he took a life, and most would think he deserved what he got. She didn't think Mary B or anyone else would understand.

"They told me you did protect yourself, is that correct? William would be proud of you for that." Mary B saw the conflicted look pass over her face. "What is it Janet? Are you feeling torn? Are you feeling like you were letting William or the family down? You are entitled to feel how you feel honey. This family is so full of dynamics, nothing is as simple as it seems. You still love him, don't you? That is okay, that just means that you have a heart and have compassion, and there is nothing wrong with that."

Janet thanked Mary B for always knowing what to say when it was needed. "So, can I ask why you didn't go to say goodbye to William at the gravesite?"

"You can, it's pretty straightforward though. I've already said my see you later to him. Plus, this ole lady is a little tired,

Christian came to make sure I was okay, but look at him, he's over there napping. I think that new lady he has is getting the better of him." Mary B chuckled as they looked over at Christian, slumbering peacefully.

Janet just laughed at that. She told Mary B that she had been to see Bo to try and find out why he did it. Mary B told Janet that it was nothing more than jealousy, he wanted what he couldn't have.

CHAPTER SEVEN

AFTER THE SERVICE DAVINA AND ROBERT WENT BACK TO Mary B's house. Davina wanted to talk to Mary B about the developments from the last few weeks. She needed advice and she knew Mary B would give it to her straight.

When they arrived, Christian was still asleep on the couch, and Mary B was lying across her bed almost asleep. "Hey Momma, how are you feeling?" Mary B told Robert she was fine and to stop babying her. Robert lay on the bed with his mom, and if one didn't know any better you would have thought he was a five-year-old again. He was his mother's son, their bond got stronger when Jean was gone.

When she returned, Robert made sure that he shared her love with his sister. It was times like these that made him realize just how much she meant to him. "Momma could Davina and I please ask your opinion on something?" Mary B looked back and forth from the two of them, anxiously.

Davina was the first to speak up, she pulled out the picture she now carried around with her, and handed it to Mary B, she explained that those are her parents. "Well I'm a hundred percent certain that is my mom, and I'm about ninety five percent sure he is my dad. There are a few problems with that though, the first of which is that I never knew him, he did some horrible things that much I know. It seems that this man may not be just a face in a picture. When Janet and I went to see Bo so she could get some answers, this man showed up. Turns out that he is Bo's father, and they are pretty close from what Janet told me. A part of me is hurt that if he is this man, that he just walked away from me, but he was there for his son. So, does that mean I'm not good enough?"

Mary B held up her hand and stopped her right there. "Davina, don't you ever let someone, and I don't care who it is, make you feel not worthy. He is the fool for ever leaving you. Davina, you have become a beautiful, smart, and talented woman. No one can take that from you. Do you understand that?"

Davina told her that she was thinking of confronting him but was unsure if he was approachable or not. She thought about going to Bo with the information but didn't know if that would cause more harm than good given his precarious mental state.

"So, what should I do?" Davina asked quietly.

"That one is a hard choice even for me. I would give it a little more time; emotions are running a bit high right now. But the only way you will know for sure is by confronting the issue. If he is willing to talk, then maybe he can offer you a reason as to why. If he isn't, that shouldn't affect him. Just make sure that Robert goes with you. Never approach a man alone, especially if you don't know what they are capable of."

Bo was healing up and they were talking about moving him to the jail. Mary B had one more step to getting the closure she needed. She asked Christian to take her to see Bo when he could find time, Christian told her anytime that she was ready they would head up to the hospital. The two of them had become quite close since William's passing. Not in a romantic way, but more in a sibling way.

Mary B never had any siblings other than her cousins growing up and Christian had been a loner also. This union was good for the both of them. They had discovered that they had a lot in common, and their love for their family was unmatched. Christian had finally gone back to work part time, he still had responsibilities around the house at Tim's. Christian still conversed with Sasha off and on, but nothing serious came of it. His time was divided between Mary B's and Jean and Tim's, and he didn't mind one bit. Mary B had spent her entire life being strong for others, so he reveled in the opportunity to be there for her.

When they arrived at the hospital, Christian went into the room with Mary B. He just stood next to the door and let her do all the talking. "Hello son, you don't know me, at least not directly. My name is Mary B; and my husband is the man who was killed a few weeks ago now."

Bo recognized her as soon as she walked in, his heart got heavy and he wanted to beg for her forgiveness at that moment, but he let her speak. He felt she deserved that modicum of respect after all that had transpired. "Yes ma'am, I was wondering if I would get to see you before the trial."

Mary B walked over close to him, she wanted to look him in the eyes as they talked. "I just want to know, why my husband? He never hurt anyone unless they bothered his family. So please, I need to know why, so that I can move on and let him go."

Bo took in a deep breath and closed his eyes for a second. *God please guide my words to give her the closure she needs,* he fervently prayed. "Ms. Mary, there is no easy answer for me to give you. I'm not a good man, I have issues that I knew about, but I refused to take the medicine to keep them under control. When I saw Janet again, I just had to have her. I had seen the man who I know now to be your husband, with her a lot. In hindsight, I guess part of that was to keep her safe from me. She also told me that she recently found out that you were family. At the time I thought what any delusional man might think that she had found another man. Yeah, I didn't pay any attention that he was much older than she. I was on a mission to get her back, the reality of it is, I don't deserve her, and I never did. I spent so much time hurting her, even when I professed to love her more than life itself. I don't expect that she will ever forgive me for what I've done; I know that I will never forgive myself. And I know it isn't much of a consolation to you ma'am, but I will plead guilty and accept whatever fate is handed down. My father thinks I'm crazy, but I feel it's the right thing to do. I have to make this as right as I can. I will never bother Janet again, but unfortunately, I will never be able to bring your beloved William back and for that I am sorry, from what Janet said he seemed like a wonderful man. But I can own up to what I have done, it's the least I could do."

Mary B's heart went out to Bo at that moment. She didn't know his whole story, not even a portion of it, but she knew William would have wanted her to forgive him. There were tears running down his face as he was talking. He wasn't scared to face her, but he was scared that she wouldn't or couldn't forgive him. In that moment she remembered what it was like to take a life and need forgiveness. Her life had been about paying penance for something she had done although she believed it to have been the only way at the time. God had showed her mercy, so therefore she would do the same.

Mary B grabbed Bo's hand and gave it a gentle squeeze; a smile crept on his face. "Son just promise me that you will get the help that you need. Whatever medicine you require, you take it. If Janet is meant for you, then she will be there for you. But you have to understand you can't put your hands on someone you profess to love and expect them to keep hanging around. Sooner or later, they will either leave or fight back. When Janet came into our lives, she was strong, yet broken. You were responsible for that. She had her tennis shoes ready to always run. She even wanted to leave town when she knew you were here, because she wanted to protect her family. We, well I, begged her to stay, she was with a family she had longed for, and we needed her just as much as she needed us, if not more. Living life on the run is no life at all. Had I allowed her to leave, William would not have died at your hands, but perhaps but some other means. You see everyone has a time to go."

"I am truly sorry ma'am. If I could do it all over I would." Bo truly felt bad about his actions.

"Well you can't do this over, but you can restart your life

from this point on. Yes, you killed my husband, and yes, I will forgive you. You, however, need to start living your life from this point with a purpose. Do something meaningful."

Just then Bo started coughing, blood starts trickling from his mouth. Mary B moves back from the bed as Christian steps in between them. He quickly presses the call button to alert the medical staff. Things begin happening too fast, Christian urges Mary B out of the room as the nurses and a doctor come rushing in.

Mary B starts praying for this young man, Christian tells her it is best that they go ahead and leave and let the medical team get him stable. "But what happened to him Christian? We were just talking and all of a sudden, he started coughing up blood."

Christian told her that he didn't know what had happened the night he was shot, or what internal damage the bullet did, so it was hard for him to know exactly what was going on. Mary B hoped that she hadn't stressed him out by having the conversation with him. Christian told her she was fine, and that whatever happened was bound to happen either way. That made Mary B feel a little better.

They watched as a nurse pushed past them with a crash cart. She headed into Bo's room. Mary B didn't want to see the young man suffer. Mistakes were made but none serious enough that required more lives to be taken. She prayed to her God to guide the hands of the doctors and nurses currently battling to save Bo's life. Christian went to the door and looked in at the mad dash of hospital personnel scrambling to save Bo's life. After a few attempts they were able to bring him back. He knew it had been a close call and told Mary B this. Her first thought was now that he had experienced death, maybe he would have a new appreciation for life. If he learned nothing else except that, in itself was a valuable lesson. Christian told Mary B that it seemed as if he would be just fine now. She simply looked up and said thank you.

CHAPTER EIGHT

DAVINA WAS BECOMING MORE AND MORE FIXATED WITH learning the truth about her father. She was determined to find out if Bobby was in fact her biological dad. Robert had told her that she had his full support no matter what she decided, and Mary B thought she should hold off just a bit until things calmed down. Davina was never one to allow someone to deter her from doing what she wanted, or thought was best. That very thinking had gotten her into trouble a time or two in the past. She decided that since she didn't live too far from the hospital, she would go up there and wait Bobby out. This plan would work until they moved Bo to the jailhouse after that she would have to revise her plan.

Vina knew she didn't have long before they did the move, judging by what Mary B had said just last night. She figured that Bobby would be there soon to see him though, given what happened just yesterday. Bo had stopped breathing for a moment while Mary B was visiting him. One of his lungs had filled up pretty extensively with blood and that was not a good sign.

While Davina was outside waiting for Bobby to show up, she heard a doctor say that she didn't know how he was still holding on. She even said that she thought he would be better off dead for taking an innocent man's life.

Davina instinctively became defensive. "Excuse me ma'am, but that isn't a very professional or nice thing to say about your patient. Yes, he took a life, but you weren't there, and you don't know the whole story or situation. So please don't judge him."

The doctor was shocked because she thought she was talking quietly, but she also hadn't realized that anyone other than the guards was sitting there. The guards had often agreed with her, so she hadn't thought much of it. The truth of the matter, she was lucky it was just a young lady who scolded her, and not someone from the board, because she would have surely lost her license.

Looking at Davina, her face turned red, "I apologize, even if that was my thoughts that was not the appropriate place or time to voice that opinion. So again, I do apologize, rest assured that in the future I will be more careful." With that haphazard apology she turned and walked away.

Davina felt a bit weird for taking up for a guy who had singlehandedly disrupted her family. At the same time, she felt like she had to defend him. She almost added, "Don't judge my brother." But she didn't know if that was being premature. When she saw him at the restaurant, she only caught a glimpse of him, she was actually too scared to look at him straight on. The stories that Janet had told her, made her feel as if he was a monster. When she looked through the window in the door at him now, he looked like a little boy. She couldn't really see his face at this angle, so she couldn't see if there was a resemblance. She didn't want to barge in on him; he didn't know who she was.

As she backed away from the door, she almost fell into Bobby. "Hey, hey slow down there. Seems like you're running from something. Definitely can't be my son, he's in no shape to hurt anyone right about now." Their eyes met, and Bobby caught his breath. He was speechless; he tried to formulate a response but couldn't find the words. She looked so much like her mother; her eyes were all his though. They were just like Bo's. A smile crossed his face; there was no denying it. She was his child. At that same moment that he realized it; Davina realized it. Bobby was indeed her dad, and that meant that Bo was her brother. She wasn't ready for what that all meant just yet.

Before Bobby could say anything, she took off running down the hall as quickly as her legs would carry her. All she could think about at that moment was Robert was going to be furious with her for going there alone. She couldn't lie to him; he knew her too well. She had promised not to lie to him since the drama with the twins. When she arrived home, Robert was waiting for her, from the look on his face it's like he knew where she was and what she was up to. "Babe, ummm..."

"Davina, just stop it. Where have you been? What have you been up to?" Robert asked, as he leaned back against the counter in their kitchen. Davina knew she had to come clean, she began telling him that she was at the hospital to try and wait for Bobby. She knew she didn't have much time, because she knew they would be moving Bo to the county jail soon as he was medically cleared. Robert had this look on his face like he couldn't believe she had done something so reckless, and alone at that. He stood there with his arms crossed across his chest, while he listened.

DAVINA CONTINUED AS IF HE WASN'T INTIMIDATING HER in the slightest. "Well Bobby did show up, and I almost fell into him. Our eyes connected and I knew without a doubt that he was my dad. I was upset when one of the doctors was standing outside his hospital room saying that Bo should just die basically. Just because he took a life doesn't automatically mean he should lose his life, she didn't know his situation, and I told her as much. She apologized but it doesn't change how she really felt. At this point I don't even know how I'm supposed to really feel about the whole thing. I mean do I take up for him like that on a regular basis. When he goes to court, am I supposed to sit on the side that is supporting him? I'm so confused. I know, I know I shouldn't have gone alone."

Robert was not saying a word, but Davina could feel his tumultuous thoughts, nonetheless. She knew his concern came from deep within his heart, he knew the things those guys were capable of doing when they felt like they were backed into a corner and he didn't trust the fact that they were born again. He wasn't leaving anything to chance, especially when it came to his family. Robert wasn't a tough guy, but he would definitely go to war over his family.

He wanted Davina to slow her pursuit, but just like with everything she did, she was moving full speed ahead. Once she put her mind to something it was hard to dissuade her. He loved and hated that about her. The phone rings, and its Janet, she tells Davina that they set a court date for two weeks for Bo. When she hung up Davina realizes that she hadn't told Janet her suspicions, and she knew she needed to before she heard them some other way.

Robert met her gaze and he nodded his head; she picked the phone up and dialed Janet's number. "Hey Janet, yeah I know we just got off the phone, but whenever you get a chance, I need to see you. You think you could come over later after you leave the hospital? I know it's a lot to ask, and I wouldn't if I had another option."

"Yeah sure, is everything okay?" Janet asked with an air of concern.

"Yeah everything is okay, I just need to talk to you about something. I will see you later."

Robert wished her luck, as he went to check in on the kids. He had been playing at a local club most nights, so he was missing some time with them. Some of the guys had asked him about joining the house band. He had to admit he was enjoying himself. He had no one to thank for this oppor-tunity but his wife, but he wanted to turn it into something that paid decently as well. Robert still felt awkward about not working for a paycheck.

Janet came over as promised a few hours later. She looked tired; she had been spending most of her time at the hospital. She wasn't giving Bo false hope of them reconciling, but just hope that he wasn't alone. She knew he needed a friend more than anything, and he willingly accepted that.

Bo had apologized time and time again over the last few weeks. He even asked her to pray with him. That was a part of him she had never seen, even the time they had gone to church together, when the pastor asked for everyone to close their eyes and bow their heads in prayer, Bo kept his eyes open and just looked straight ahead. Janet was happy that he was coming to terms with what happened and forgiving himself. It wasn't the easiest thing in the world for her to forgive him, but she knew she couldn't hold onto that hatred forever. She had lost so much time already living in fear, she wasn't ready to give up any more of her time on this earth wondering about the what ifs.

Davina had been kind of weird when she had called earlier. As far as Janet knew there wasn't anything going on with the family, at least Mary B hadn't said anything when she spoke to her earlier. Robert opened the door for her with the twins wrapped around him. She hadn't been over as much because of all that had happened, so she missed all of that energy that they had. She hugged Robert tightly, she had missed seeing him too. They all had become close before their world blew up right in front of their eyes.

Davina was waiting for Janet in the living room. She had the few pictures that she had of her mom and dad out on the table. Janet noticed that Davina was looking tired and stressed and she looked like she had been crying recently. She went to Davina and hugged her like she hadn't seen her in years. They had grown as close as sisters, especially when they were working together during Davina's rehab. "What is going on with you baby girl?"

Davina didn't know where to start, "Look at these pictures. Have I ever shown them to you? They are pictures of my mom and of my dad, well at least the man I think is my dad. Does he look familiar to you?" Davina waited before she continued on, she knew that she was throwing a bit much at Janet all at once, but she didn't know how else to say it other than just saying it. Janet looked at the pictures like he was familiar, but not as if she knew him exactly.

"What I'm about to say is going to be crazy, but I believe Bo is my brother. Not only that, I believe we share the same dad. He is our connection. The guy that's in this picture his name is Bobby, Bo's dad name is Bobby. When I ran into him at the hospital earlier, I knew it was him, and I think he realized who I was too. I was there alone and so I just took off. I thought I was ready to face him, but I really wasn't. So now I'm confused and torn. I don't know if I'm supposed to take up for a brother who tried to kill my cousin and who killed my father in law. I defended him earlier when a doctor was being insensitive, it felt like the thing to do. It felt right. I mean I didn't do it because he could hear me, or I gained anything from it because I didn't, but it felt like I was somehow being untrue to William. Afterwards I could see William smiling at me saying, "That's my girl". I know he wouldn't want me to be unforgiving because that's not the type of man he was. Somehow, I don't think that even William could have predicted that he was my brother though. Please say something to stop my incessant rambling here."

Janet was taken by surprise by the information that she just received. Looking at Davina now, there was a bit Bo in her, they had the same eyes and nose. She had never noticed it before. They were both stubborn, but she had never imagined that they were related. Bo never mentioned that he was from N.C, he had only made his way down south within the last few years. So much was going through her mind it felt like her entire world had shifted on its axis once more. Did he know Davina was his sister? Did Bobby know about Davina all this time? Why didn't she know about any of this? Was there anything else she didn't know? Just when she didn't think things could get any weirder, something else happens. "Who all knows about this? And for those who don't know when were you planning to bring it up before or after court?"

Davina told her the only ones who knew about it was just her, Mary B, and Robert. As to when she would confront him, she hadn't gotten that far. She didn't anticipate that it would be before the court date though. It was all still too new, and the wounds were still fresh.

Jean hadn't taken things as well as everyone else, most of the others had been able to forgive Bo because they knew in the end William would have wanted them to do just that, she just couldn't bring herself to find forgiveness at that point. Tim, being her man and protector, stood strong and by her side with her choice. Davina didn't want to be the reason that the family stood divided during the trial, but she felt by her knowing what she did that was going to be the case. The more she thought about it, she realized she might just have to bring it up before court. Lord help them all if she did.

CHAPTER NINE

Janet, feeling overwhelmed with this revelation from Davina, wasn't sure whether she needs to talk to Bo and find out the truth, or even if he knows the truth. She heads straight to Mary B's after she leaves Davina's. If there was one place, she knew she could get some unbiased advice it is there. Janet never imagined that when she came to work with Davina and this family that things would turn out so entangled and such a mess. The more comfortable she feels with getting to know them as family, the deeper and more twisted things seem to be. The crazy part is Janet knows she only knows a small portion of this family's history.

Upon arriving at Mary B's, Christian is pulling up as well. Janet jokes, "It looks like I must be in time for dinner."

Christian laughed, "Don't be interrupting my dinner date with my lovely Mary. You know these are the nights I live for." Christian caught the anguished look on Janet's face. He immediately began asking if everything was okay. She shook her head and headed into the house.

Mary B was waiting, as if she knew someone needed her.

She had been having a hard time finding reasons to get out of bed some days, she missed her William so. "Come in Janet, what is troubling you? You know I can tell when things are wrong? And I see there is a struggle going on inside of you. Tell me what has you in such turmoil?"

Janet tells her about the pictures of Davina's mom and dad. "Mary, what if Bo's father is actually her father? Do you know how that must make her feel? None of this would be happening if I had just left when I started to, this ripple effect from my one decision has changed our family forever."

Mary B chose her words as carefully as she could. "Janet, sweet, sweet Janet, so much has happened since we first met. None of it is something I would change. If they share the same father so what? That isn't something you can control. If anything, her knowing will give her a sense of closure one way or the other. Yes, it is another adjustment for the family to get through, but we always do, and we do it together. My Davina has always tried to appear that she didn't need anyone, and, in most cases, she has probably been right, except for now she will need you as a friend standing resolutely by her side through this difficult time. The trial no matter what way it goes, she will be conflicted then too. One side is because she feels a sense of loyalty to our family, and us and the other is for a family she never had. Sometimes blood is thicker than love."

Just then Christian offered up some words to her, as he had been listening from the kitchen. "You do know Mary is right. No matter what happens, this family is here for you." He smiles a bit, "Yeah I know I have only been in it a minute myself, but there is no place I would rather be. They have taken me in and treated me like family and I adore me some Mary B."

"Alright now, cut that out before you make my William start haunting you for being fresh with his Mary B." Mary B offered a slight chuckle as she moved around offering refreshments.

Janet couldn't help but smile at that thought herself. She remembered William's gentle smile all too well and hated that she would never see it again. He above everyone else was always good to her, he protected her as if she was his own flesh and blood and that was something she never had. Immediately her smile turned into tears. Mary B understood that it was the thoughts of William causing her tears this time and decided to give her a little breathing room so she could calm down on her own. She needed time to figure out what if anything she needed to do with this information, but she knew she needed to keep Vina in the loop no matter what, and she didn't want to stir the pot before Davina had a chance to process her feelings on the matter and make peace with her decision, the way she needed to.

Davina couldn't sleep, she tossed and turned. She hadn't meant to upset Janet by telling her about Bobby, but she just wanted to make sure she knew it was possible. Davina had spent her time trying to fit in. She had wanted a family, but not at a cost that would rock the core of the one she had established. Robert tried to calm her and reassure her that no matter what happened they would be all right. She dreamt of a faceless man that night, he was belligerent and screaming at her mom. That's all she could remember when she woke up, but she felt deep down that it was some repressed memory of Bobby.

BOBBY COULDN'T EVEN LIE; HE WAS SHAKEN UP FROM seeing the young lady that close up again. There was no denying it now, he got a full head on look at her, and that had to be his child. The resemblance of her mother and of him was uncanny. He tried to shake the feeling as he entered Bo's hospital room. Bobby needed Bo to know he had his full attention no matter what. Flashes of Davina kept entering his mind as if on replay, he was only half listening to his son. Again, he tries to pull himself together, and listen as his son is talking.

"Dad! Dad? Are you even listening to me? Are you okay? What is going on? I have never seen you act this way in my life but something or someone has you shook up, or is it spooked? Either way I know something is not right. So, talk to me, you know we don't have much time before they try and transfer me." Bo was becoming frustrated with his dad.

"Are they still planning on moving you even though you almost died a few days ago?"

Bo nodded. He was sad because he knew he wouldn't be able to see Janet on a regular basis once he was moved. He knew that she wasn't obligated to see him, but she had been coming pretty steadily and he liked it. Bo wasn't getting it confused, he knew Janet didn't want him but yet she was still there for him, and for now that was enough. He remembered what the old lady had said, if it's meant to be it will be.

A smile crossed his face. Bobby noticed it and inquired. "What's going on with you and that goofy smile?" Bo waved his dad off, well he tried to anyway, he finally told him that he had been thinking about Janet, and he looked at his father's face to gauge his reaction.

"See, I knew you were not listening when I was talking before. I know she isn't for me, at least not for now. I know in order to get her back I've got some work to do. But I've got work to do for myself above all else. I have so much to work on it is crazy, but I have to, I killed an innocent man, and almost the woman I love. I need help Dad."

Bobby reached over and hugged his son for the first time in a while. "I'm always here for you no matter what, son; you are the better parts of me." Just then the girl flashed in his head and she wouldn't leave. He kept trying to blink her away, but images of her and her mother just wouldn't leave. "Bo, I've got to go for now, but I will see you soon. We have something to talk about, but there are some things I have to work out first. Always know that I love you and I am proud of you. I'm proud to be your father."

There was that uneasy feeling with his dad again, and the look in his eyes was of real concern. Bo let his father leave without holding him up; it had to be something important to make his father so worried.

Bobby couldn't get out of the hospital soon enough. He needed to get some air, that's all it was. He simply needed to clear his head. His heart was racing. This girl's sudden appearance has his mind bugging. He knew that she was his, but it's like she is haunting him all of a sudden. Bobby decides he needs to blow off some steam, so instead of heading back to the hotel, he heads to one of the local clubs.

Given Bobby's past this may not have been his best plan, he was well aware of that, but he didn't know how else to get the girl out of his thoughts. He hadn't thought about her, truly thought about her in years, but seeing her must have been too much for even him. He knew he should never have come back here, but what were the chances of physically running into her? She shouldn't even be here, a few drinks should help him clear his head, it usually does.

HE COULD HEAR THE MUSIC PLAYING BEFORE HE entered the door. The club he chose wasn't one of the booty shaking ones, but rather one of those that played that neo soul kind of jazz. On the way into the club he stopped to buy a dime bag from a hood on the corner. He smiled to himself as he entered, "Oh yeah, this is just what I needed." Bobby finds himself a corner and orders a beer; he lights up his blunt and begins to feel a little mellow. His mind was at ease just like he needed it to be, so much so that he didn't pay attention to the guy watching him from the stage.

Robert only saw the photos that his wife had been freaking out over since his father's death, but he knew without a doubt that this was the man in the picture. Robert was being careful not to draw attention to himself and get caught staring. He had a sudden distaste for this man that left his wife as a child. Bobby was too lost to the music and his blunt that he just closed his eyes to let the music take him to a place where he could forget about the girl at least for a little while. Surprisingly, he drifts off to sleep.

Robert had sent a waitress over to try and see if she could get him to talk, but he wasn't interested. Robert was intent on watching him and trying to learn whatever he could about this guy. So far, he seems normal, but he did seem pretty agitated when he came in. Robert hadn't seen someone come in the club to go to sleep before. There he stayed, until the waitress went to wake him and tell him it was closing time. He still was a little irritated, but he left without a fuss, all the while Robert just watched.

That night as Robert was leaving the club, he was debating whether or not to tell Davina, but then he realized he didn't really have much to tell her at this point. He knew he didn't really want to get her all riled up, or worse yet trying to stake out the club in case he came back. Robert would never forgive himself if something happened to her. He knew this whole thing meant a lot to her, and he wanted her to have some closure. In the end he decided this encounter he would keep to himself, at least for now.

CHAPTER TEN

BOBBY MADE IT TO HIS CAR AND WAS ABOUT TO DRIVE off, when he noticed two police cars parked across the street. He took a deep breath and started the car. He shouldn't be jumpy, but he knew his past could still catch up to him. Matter of fact, he has been waiting for it to happen. It would only be fitting he thought, after everything that has happened to bring him back to this place, he left in the wind a long time ago. It's funny no matter how much time has passed he still straightens up and his nerves get the best of him when he sees an officer.

Bobby knows it is just his conscious pricking him over past sins. He had to admit that since he seen the girl, he has been more nervous than he had been in many years. Without knowing it, she has the power to destroy this life that he had built. When he slept that night, he had a dream of not the girl, but of his days when he was in the drug and prostitution game. He thought about all the things he had done to the girls himself, as well as what he allowed to happen, all for drugs and money. Bobby promised himself that Bo would not ever know about that part of his world, although he felt that was a promise, he wasn't going to be able to keep the longer he was in this town.

The dream on this night was different, he saw the girl as one of the girls he helped hold captive. When he woke up, he was gasping for air. He knew without a doubt that he would kill someone if something like that happened to his child. Just the thought made Bobby's stomach turn. He wished he could just leave this place never to return but he couldn't abandon his son, not now.

THE NEXT TIME HE CLOSED HIS EYES HE SAW ANOTHER face; one he hadn't seen since he left that building many years ago. It was the face of the one girl who he himself repeatedly raped and would only share her when it was good business. He remembered her face was so sweet and young at the time. She was special to him, as special as he would allow someone to be back then. He couldn't believe some guy gave her up to him for some coke. She was worth so much more.

He had people constantly requesting her, and he made the choice as to who touched this one. She wouldn't break as the others had before her. He remembered that she had a strong will and would fight them off her every chance she got. He admitted to himself she suffered a lot because of it, all she had to do was just do what she was told. Bobby told her if she just did what she was told that he would give her the drugs she desired, all she had to do was be good. Even when she got pregnant, his clients still begged for her. That knowledge seemed to have excited them even more. Bobby didn't know who the father of the child was; but he knew he had a buyer for it, if it survived.

That was going to be a first for him, selling babies, but he figured it couldn't be much different than dealing with women. He never got the chance to execute his plan, there was an raid and police were everywhere, he saw most of his friends killed. As shots rang out, he took off, constantly looking over his shoulder. That was when he vowed to leave that place behind and never return, yet here he was, right back in the thick of things.

He was supposed to have been there when everything went down, but at the last minute someone called and wanted some drugs, so instead of sending one of his errand boys, he chose to deliver it himself. That decision saved his life. Shaking his head, he didn't understand why he dreamt of her, he hadn't thought about her in years. She was just another body, and that was the beginning of Bobby's unraveling. He just didn't know it. He needed this mess with Bo to get settled and soon.

Over the next few weeks he fell into a routine, he would visit his son during the day and at night he would hit up that little nightspot. He was digging the music and the laid-back atmosphere, not to mention there was a waitress who kept checking on him. Bo's transfer had been pushed back because of what had happened. They wanted to make sure he was stable and would be able to stand trial, and handle the transfer before they moved him.

Bobby was thankful, but that just meant he was going to be here for a little longer than planned. He could tell that Bo sensed his uneasiness, but he kept telling his son that he was just concerned about him. That first night Bobby went to the club he fell asleep. He laughed at himself because he knew that wasn't normal. The waitress told him that after a few more visits. Since then he would only light up and drink a maximum of three drinks, and just listen to the music. Tianna, the waitress had gotten used to this guy coming in regularly now, plus he was a good tipper. She remembered his order and brought it over without him asking. Bobby thought to himself, he could get used to this.

The music was playing softly in the background and Bobby lit up his second blunt for the night. Tianna had brought him over his third beer for the evening. He was feeling relaxed and as if he didn't have a care in the world. Little did he know his past and present were about to collide.

DAVINA AND JANET HAD DECIDED A COUPLE WEEKS AGO that they needed a lady's night out. The last few months had taken its toll on them both and they just wanted to cut loose, have a few drinks, and relax. Davina suggested they hit up the club that Robert was playing at.

She had resisted going there because she wanted him to be himself and enjoy making music. He needed his outlet as much as the next. She hoped this wasn't a mistake. Davina hadn't told him before he left to head to the club that she and Janet may show up. She only told him, she and Janet were going to hang out for a bit.

"Davina are you sure Robert is going to be okay with us crashing his spot?" Janet asked as they were walking to the door.

Prior to Janet asking the question Davina felt confident

that all would be fine. Now there was an uneasiness that settled in the pit of her stomach. Maybe they should change their destination or stay home altogether.

Just then Kaloni, yelled out "Momma! Momma!" At that moment all of Davina's hesitation went out the window.

"Janet, we are going, and we are going to have fun. We deserve to get away and just recharge for a bit."

Janet caved easily enough, she was exhausted from everything, not to mention she had been driving back and forth between Mary B's and Davina's weekly. For some reason she just couldn't deal with being alone. She always felt like she was waiting for the other shoe to drop.

The family consistently reassured her, that Bo could no longer hurt her. Deep down she knew he was getting some help and he couldn't hurt her at this point, but there was this lingering feeling. Without noticing Janet had gotten lost in her thoughts.

"Snap out of it, Janet." Davina was waving her hand in front of Janet's face, trying to pull her out of her morose thoughts.

"Ok ok, no need to yell at me." Janet laughed as they walked down the front walkway and out to Davina's car.

"WOULD YOU LIKE ANOTHER DRINK SUGA?" TIANNA asked Bobby. She rarely spoke to him beyond normal pleasantries; he didn't make her feel like conversation was welcome. Tianna still couldn't help but think, he wasn't a bad looking guy for an older guy. Bobby avoided making too much eye contact with Tianna or anyone for that matter. He did find her very appealing. It had been a long time since he was with a woman. But it seemed as if any time he got involved with a woman that was when bad things happened.

Without thinking he shook his head. Tianna was about to walk away but, he reached out and grabbed her arm. "No, the head shake wasn't for you. My sincere apologies for grabbing your wrist, I hope I didn't hurt you."

Tianna smiled, "No, you are fine. What would you like to drink? Another of the same?" This was a first for him. Tianna knew he always tapped out at drink number three.

"Yes please. Thanks for always taking care of me when I'm here. I do appreciate it." Bobby tried to smile as he said it. But the expression just ended up looking weird. Tianna just attributed it to the fact he was a little high.

She walked away to go grab his drink, along with some buffalo flavored wings. He had ordered them before, and she knew he was about to have his fourth drink, so he needed something on his stomach.

Robert kept his gaze onto the guy he had been watching for weeks now. Robert was contemplating working his nerve up to approach him. He just didn't know how to do it or what he would say. He noticed there was more conversation between the man and Tianna tonight than usual. Robert made a mental note to speak to her about it later tonight and hopped off the stage to take a restroom break before the next set started.

On the way back from the restaurant he stopped by the bar to get a cranberry juice and seltzer water. He thought it would be hard working at the club, while everyone else was drinking and smoking, but it was easier than he thought.

Knowing he had to be better for his family made it worth it. Robert was determined not to go down that dark road again.

Isabelle the bartender smiled and said to Robert, "You are playing great tonight as always Robert. You really should invite your wife soon. We would love to finally meet her."

This is something Robert had been hearing more and more over the last few weeks. Between the club owner, Joseph and several of the others, they often joked he only wore the ring to throw women off. That was until Joseph called him at home to see if he could come in early and play for a party. Davina answered the phone, taking Joseph by surprise. So much so that he invited her to stop by any time after he asked for Robert. That night at the club, he announced Davina was real. The staff looked as if they were shocked. They cut him some slack after that point.

Smiling as he returned to his seat about to play his next set, his eyes darted to the front door. The smile drained from his face as he saw Davina enter. She immediately scanned the room and locked eyes with Robert. Janet eased by Davina who stopped dead in her tracks when she saw the stunned look on Robert's face it concerned her. It was almost as if he was horrified.

He immediately made his way over to her, careful to keep his eyes on Bobby. Just as Robert reached the ladies, Janet spoke up, "Oh no! Davina we should go. I don't think this was the best night for us to come out." Janet had surveyed the room and spotted Bobby sitting in the corner.

· · ·

DAVINA FOLLOWED THE DIRECTION JANET'S EYES drifted looking in Bobby's direction. He was in his own world; he hadn't noticed the women enter. Before Robert could reach for Davina's hand, she was making her way over to where Bobby was sitting. As she approached the table, Bobby tried to focus in on her. He didn't do it quick enough in order to react. He blinked and she was there.

"Davina, babe, what are you doing here?" Robert asked as he hurried through the crowd and pulled her to him.

"We came to listen to you play. We needed a night out. Maybe more than I realized."

Looking from Robert to Bobby, Davina asked, "Do you know this man Robert?"

Robert shook his head in response, he dared not speak a lie to his wife. Davina starred him down. "No babe, not really. We've never met. He just comes in club sometimes."

BOBBY HAD BEEN SITTING THERE JUST LISTENING, AT one point thinking they might forget he was there and move on. That didn't happen, so he interjected. "Listen, you guys are blowing my high." He thought if he played it off coolly, they would walk away. Even though in his mind, he knew he would have to face this part of his past. There was no escaping it.

Davina took the opportunity to slip into the vacant chair across from Bobby. "Can I ask your name?"

"You already know who I am. What is it that you want from me?"

Davina could tell he was high, and probably a little drunk as he was slurring his words.

Davina couldn't answer Bobby. There was so many things going through her mind, but nothing came from her mouth. Over the last few months she had nightmares and dreams about this very moment. What would happen if their paths crossed? Now that the moment was upon her, she was stunned silent.

Robert extended his hand to Bobby. "Look man, forgive my family for the interruption. But since we are here, I'm Robert, this is my wife Davina, and this is my cousin Janet."

Bobby extended his hand to Robert. "I'm Bobby. I know you have questions, but tonight isn't the night for me to answer them."

AFTERWORD

Thank You for Reading....

Don't forget to sign up for
Mind Flow Publishing & Production LLC's Newsletter @
www.mindflowpublishingproduction.com

Email us for autographed or additional paperback copies @
mindflowpubpro@gmail.com

Other Titles Also Available Include

Mental Interlude --- Poetry
The Mary B Chronicles 1 & 2 --- Fiction
Journey to Living (Kindle Only) --- Inspirational
Simple Complexity --- Poetry
Spoken From The Heart --- Poetry
Dreams Do Come True (Kindle Only) --- Fiction
Charisma's Homecoming --- Fiction

For Her Love --- Fiction

Available Through
Amazon
Barnes & Noble
Kindle

Coming Soon

Freedom In The Cage Series --- Fiction
A Love For Holly --- Cozy Romance
A Prince For Me --- Romantic Comedy

Upcoming Titles Will Be Available
Through
Amazon
Barnes & Noble
Kindle
Apple iBooks
Kobo

ABOUT THE AUTHOR

Although I'm still considered new to the publishing world, I have hit the ground running full speed ahead. In my first year, I was signed to Mind Flow Publishing & Production LLC, and I have published a total of 6 books. I have earned Amazon's Best Sellers Top 100 orange banner. My works are spread across several genres such as; Poetry, Inspirational, Urban Fiction and Christian Fiction. I will be trying my hand at cozy mysteries, romance, and sci-fi. My love for writing started when I was about 12, writing poetry and writing speeches for various oratorical contests. Inspiration for my craft is pulled from my own life experiences, as well as others. I have been featured on several podcasts, as well as Up and Coming Authors Newsletters. When I'm not writing, I love to design shadowboxes, and create personalized greeting cards. I have released my 3rd poetry book (Spoken from the Heart) in August 2019. Current books available are The Mary B Chronicles 1 & 2, Mental Interlude, and Journey to Living, Simple Complexity, and Dreams Do Come True, Spoken from the Heart, and Charisma's Homecoming. All of which are available on Amazon, and www. mindflowpublishingproduction.com.

www.ingramcontent.com/pod-product-compliance
Lightning Source LLC
Chambersburg PA
CBHW072036170626
46811CB00008B/3093